AURA

This edition reprinted in 2014 by Baker & Taylor UK Ltd, Bicester, Oxfordshire.
Licensed exclusively to Top That Publishing Ltd
Tide Mill Way, Woodbridge, Suffolk, IP12 1AP, UK
www.topthatpublishing.com
Copyright © 2014 Tide Mill Media
All rights reserved
2 4 6 8 9 7 5 3 1
Printed and bound in China

Creative Director – Simon Couchman
Editorial Director – Daniel Graham

Written by Clement C. Moore
Illustrated by Marcin Nowakowski

ISBN 978-1-78244-415-2

A catalogue record for this book is available from the British Library
Printed and bound in China

'Twas the Night Before Christmas

An adaptation of
Clement C. Moore's famous poem

'Twas the night before Christmas,
when all through the house

Not a creature was stirring,
not even a mouse.

The stockings were hung
by the chimney with care,

In hopes that St Nicholas
soon would be there.

My sister and I were nestled
all snug in our beds,

While visions of sugar-plums
danced in our heads.

And mamma in her pyjamas,
and father in his cap,

Had just settled down for
a long winter's nap.

When out on the lawn
there arose such a clatter,

I sprang from the bed
to see what was the matter.

Away to the window
I flew like a flash,

Tore open the curtains
and threw up the sash.

The moon shining onto
the new-fallen snow
Gave the lustre of midday
to objects below.

When, what to my wondering eyes
should appear,
But a bright red sleigh,
and eight bright-eyed reindeer.

With a jolly old driver, so lively and quick,
I knew in a moment it must be St Nick.

More rapid than eagles
his reindeer they came,
And he whistled, and shouted,
and called them by name!

'Now Dasher!
Now, Dancer!
Now, Prancer
and Vixen!

On, Comet!
On, Cupid!
On, Donner
and Blitzen!

To the top of the porch!
To the top of the wall!

Now dash away! Dash away!

As dry leaves that before
    the wild hurricane fly,

When they meet with an obstacle,
    rising up in the sky.

        So up to the house-top
        the reindeers they flew,

With the sleigh full of toys,
and St Nicholas too.

Then, in a twinkling,
I heard on the roof

The prancing and pawing
of each reindeer hoof.

As I drew in my head,
and was turning around,

Down the chimney
St Nicholas came
with a bound.

He was dressed all in red,
from his head to his foot,

And his clothes were all tarnished
with ashes and soot.

A bundle of toys
he had flung on his back,

And he looked like a peddler,
just opening his pack.

His eyes – how they twinkled!
His dimples, how merry!

His cheeks were like roses,
his nose like a cherry!

His friendly mouth was
drawn up like a bow,

And the beard of his chin
was as white as the snow.

He had a broad face
and a little round belly,

That shook when he laughed,
like a bowl full of jelly!

He was chubby and plump,
a right jolly old elf,

And I laughed when I saw him,
in spite of myself!

A wink of his eye
and a twist of his head,

Soon let me know
I had nothing to dread.

He spoke not a word,
but went straight to his work,

And filled all the stockings,
then turned with a jerk.

And laying his finger
on the side of his nose,

And giving a nod,
up the chimney he rose!

He sprang to his sleigh,
to his team gave a whistle,

And away they all flew
like the seeds of a thistle.

But I heard him exclaim,
before he drove out of sight,

'Happy Christmas to all,

and to all a good-night!'